JOHNNY APPLESEED

by
Carol Beach York

illustrated by
Joan Goodman

Folk Tales of America

Troll Associates

PROLOGUE

John Chapman earned the name of Johnny
Appleseed. He is one American folk hero who
was a real person. He was born in Leominster,
Massachusetts, on September 26, 1774, and he
died near Fort Wayne, Indiana, in March of
1845.

We know about Johnny Appleseed through
stories told over the years, about his kindness
to people and animals, about his cheerful
nature, about his love of the wilderness. Each
time these stories are retold, they speak of a
real person who became a real folk hero.

Library of Congress # 79-66312
ISBN 0-89375-296-7/0-89375-295-9 (pb)

Any time you bite into an apple, you should think about Johnny Appleseed.

That wasn't his real name. His real name was John Chapman. He got his nickname because he planted apple seeds—oh, not just a *few* apple seeds. *Hundreds* of apple seeds. *Thousands* of apple seeds. Maybe a *million*. Some folks say when he was born, he came right out of the ground with a sack of apple seeds over his shoulder.

The true fact is he was born just like every other baby. But maybe he liked apples better than most.

Johnny was born a long time ago, before the Declaration of Independence was signed, when America was still a group of English colonies. His father was a Massachusetts farmer, and Johnny liked to help around the farm, especially in the apple orchard. He liked to climb up in an apple tree, pick off a juicy red apple to eat, polish it on his shirt sleeve, and enjoy every bite.

Where young Johnny lived there were farms and orchards and towns. And for a while he thought the whole world was like Massachusetts.

But the country was growing, spreading out to the west. Settlers were moving to far places where the only roads were Indian trails, where there were no towns or stores or schools or even houses to live in. The pioneers had to build their own houses—which weren't much at first, just rough log cabins. They also had to clear fields and plant crops. So, they didn't have time for such things as planting orchards and raising fruit trees.

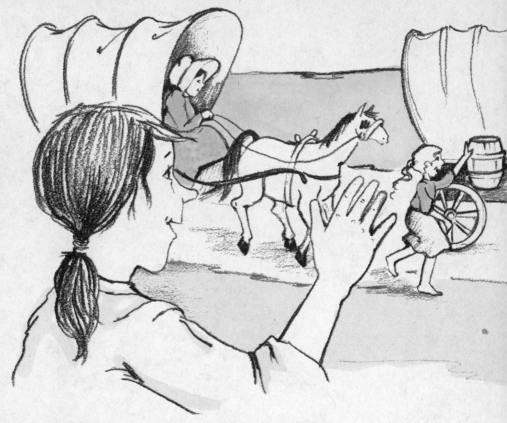

"No fruit trees? Not even apple trees?"
Johnny could hardly believe his ears when he
heard about *that*.

Johnny often saw the pioneer wagons pass-
ing his farm on their way to new land in the
Ohio Valley. Sometimes a single wagon, sometimes a small string of wagons traveled together.

Women in sunbonnets and gingham dresses
waved from the wagon seats.

Barefoot children shouted as they ran along in the road.

Dogs barked and wheels creaked as the wagons swayed under their heavy loads.

Johnny watched the pioneers and thought about the hard and often lonely life they would have, building cabins and clearing forest land. He was sorry they wouldn't see beautiful pink apple blossoms in springtime or have piping hot apple tarts for Sunday dinner.

"I'd like to give every family an apple tree to take to Ohio," Johnny thought.

But the settlers' wagons were already full-to-spilling-over with things they needed. Clothes and food. Seeds for crops. Farm tools. Dishes and bits of furniture for their new homes. Even if Johnny could have dug up an apple tree, even if it would have lived through the long journey, there was no way the settlers could take it with them.

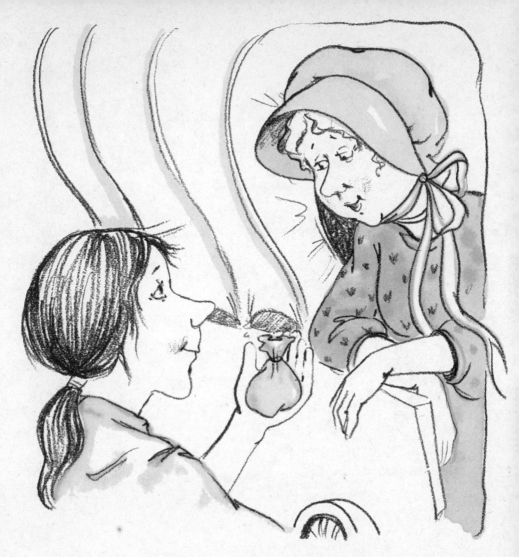

The next best thing Johnny could think of was to give seeds to the settlers. So whenever he ate an apple, he saved the seeds. He sewed them into leather pouches and gave them to the people bound for Ohio. Somehow, he hoped, they would get at least a few apple trees planted and tended and raised.

12

"You've got to put up a fence after you plant the seeds," he told the settlers. "Deer like to nibble the shoots when the trees start to grow. And you've got to keep weeds from choking off the seedlings."

The settlers looked a little doubtful that they would have time for all this. They had so much to do, making a new life in a new place.

But Johnny knew all about planting, tending, and raising apple trees. One day the idea came to him that he could go to the Ohio Valley himself and plant apple orchards for the settlers.

"That's an outlandish idea if I ever heard one," his Pa said. He couldn't understand why Johnny would want to leave his comfortable home, his family, and his friends.

"I want to help the settlers," Johnny told him. "And I know all about apple trees."

Johnny's mother didn't take to the idea any faster than Johnny's Pa.

"You can't just go off into the wilderness by yourself," she said. "Think of the wild animals. Think of the snowstorms. And where would you sleep?"

"Why, I'll sleep right out under the sky," Johnny said. "The sky is the best roof anyone can have over him."

"It might be pretty," said Johnny's mother, "but it won't keep off much rain."

Johnny laughed. "I don't mind rain. Rain helps things grow."

"That's true," Pa agreed.

And it was true.

Johnny's mother was still worried. But when she could see that he was set in his mind to go, she made him a good warm coat. She packed food for him to take, and she gave up her best cooking pan, so he could kindle fires and have warm meals as he traveled.

Just before he left, Johnny went to the cider mill a few miles from his farm. He asked for some apple seeds.

The cider mill used more apples than you could count, but they didn't use the seeds— which was pretty good sense. Not too many people liked to drink cider with seeds floating around in it!

"Take all the seeds you want," the men at the cider mill told Johnny.

When Johnny walked back home, his
mother had the food and the warm coat and
the cooking pan all packed. Johnny's knapsack
was stuffed full. There wasn't enough space
left to squeeze in a dried bean, let alone a big
load of apple seeds.

Johnny's mother pushed and pulled and re-
packed. But there was still no room.

Johnny's Pa scratched his whiskers and
frowned.

"I'll just have to do without something," Johnny said.

"You've got to have a warm coat. Cold weather's coming on," Johnny's mother told him. "And you've got to have food. And you've got to have a pan to cook it in."

Everybody looked at the bulging knapsack.

Johnny knew that his mother and father were sad to see him go, and he wanted to make them laugh. So he pulled the cooking pan out of the sack and plunked it on his head. "I'll just wear my cooking pan," he said.

He did look pretty funny with a pan for a hat, and the handle sticking out behind. His Pa began to laugh.

"If you don't look a sight," Johnny's mother said. She began to laugh, too.

Then they waved goodbye to Johnny as he started off for the Ohio Valley, which was a far piece away!

It wasn't an easy trip. Johnny walked hundreds of miles with his apple seeds and his cooking pan and his warm coat. But he was

never sorry he had set out. He whistled as he walked, and he made friends everywhere, even before he got to the Ohio Valley. He had to walk right across the state of Pennsylvania, and he made friends with people in farmhouses along the way.

Sometimes he stopped and helped a farmer mend a harness or chop firewood. When the farmers asked where he was going, Johnny always said, "I'm on my way to Ohio to plant apple trees. I want to help the settlers."

The families would put an extra plate on the table for Johnny. They gave him food to take with him when he was ready to go on his way again.

Johnny liked the out-of-doors. He liked sleeping under the stars. And his mother needn't have worried about the wild animals. Johnny got along with all of them just fine. Even the bears.

Indeed, there were bears in the forests Johnny walked through—bears with great, lumbering, furry bodies and strong claws. Bears bigger than Johnny was!

One time, when Johnny was nearly all the way to Ohio, it began to snow. At first he didn't know it was going to be quite such a blizzard. He was in a deep part of the forest, and there was no trail to follow. But Johnny wasn't worried. He had never lost his way in a forest yet. He was sure he wouldn't get lost just because of a little snow.

But it wasn't long before Johnny could see that this wasn't just "a little snow." Flakes were flying thicker than feathers from a busted pillow. Pretty soon Johnny was walking in snow up to his ankles.

Then up to his knees.

He couldn't see anything but snow in front of him, around him, behind him.

There wasn't much use plodding through snow that was piling up higher and faster than he could walk. Johnny couldn't see *anything*. Then he stumbled over a fallen log and fell flat. After he picked himself up out of the snow, he peered into the log. It was hollow and big enough for a bear to crawl into. There was no doubt about that, because a bear *had* crawled into the log and was sound asleep.

But there was enough room left for Johnny. He crawled right in next to the bear and rested until the blizzard was over.

The bear opened one eye and took a look. Then he went back to sleep. He didn't mind Johnny being in his log. But it's likely the bear never had such a thing happen before or since. Most folks don't want to snuggle up to bears much.

Years later, tales were told about Johnny
and the forest creatures. People said wild deer
ate right out of his hand. Birds lighted on his
shoulders. Wolves and foxes were as tame as
barn cats around Johnny.

No snake would bite him.

No bee would sting him.

No rabbit was frightened into a hole when
Johnny came walking by.

"Squirrels dig up their acorns to share with
him," folks said.

After the snowy night in the bear's log in the forest, Johnny came to the Ohio Valley. Just as he had made friends all along the way through Pennsylvania, Johnny was making friends in the Ohio Valley faster than you can say APPLESAUCE.

He planted his apple seeds along the river banks.

First, he scratched holes with a pointed stick. Then he dropped the seeds into the holes. When the seeds were planted, he piled up bushes to make sturdy, prickly fences to protect the tiny saplings when they began to grow.

Then he would move on to another place and plant more seeds.

But he always came back to weed and care for the young shoots of the apple trees.

When the seedlings were strong enough, and about a foot high, Johnny would dig them up. He gave them to pioneer families so they could have orchards in the years to come.

One pioneer woman didn't know an apple tree when she saw one.

"What's *that*?" she asked, when Johnny came to her doorway with an armful of scrawny twigs.

"Why, these are apple trees," Johnny said. "In a few years you'll have apples to bake, apples for pies, and apples for jelly."

The pioneer woman began to look a bit more interested in the spindly sticks with roots and clumps of dirt dangling at the ends.

"In the spring you'll see pink apple blossoms," Johnny promised. "There's not a prettier sight anywhere."

He planted the trees near the cabin, so the woman could see the blossoms in the springtime when the trees were grown.

Then he carried seedling trees to the next cabin.

And the next.

The first little apple orchards began to grow in the Ohio Valley.

Johnny was helping to make the new land beautiful, and he helped the settlers in other ways, too. He pulled up stumps and planted corn. He even built furniture for the cabins.

The settlers set an extra place at the table whenever Johnny came by, just as they had done when he traveled through Pennsylvania. He was a favorite guest.

"Wash up, children. Suppertime—Johnny Appleseed's having supper with us tonight!"

The children would scurry. They wanted to hear the tales Johnny told after supper, when the family gathered around the fireplace. Rocking chairs creaked and flames crackled. The children lay on their stomachs on the

cabin floor and listened to Johnny tell about his travels, about the animals who were his friends in the forest, about the bear in the log.

Then, when it was growing late, Johnny would wind up the evening by reading from his Bible.

"It's news straight from heaven," he always said.

Everyone would listen to his gentle voice reading the joyful words from the worn, old book he loved so much.

The next day he would be gone, planting seeds, tending new trees.

Whenever Johnny ran out of seeds, he would make the long trek back to the cider mills in Pennsylvania and fill up his sack again. How many miles he walked each year! If anybody was giving prizes for walking, Johnny Appleseed would have won them all!

As he traveled up and down the countryside, planting seeds and helping the settlers, he also carried news from cabin to cabin.

"You're as good as a newspaper," the settlers told him. They were in such a new and lonely place that they rarely even heard news of neighbors a few miles away. But Johnny brought news from everywhere.

One of the things the settlers always wanted news about was the Indians. The Shawnee lived right there in the Ohio Valley at that time, close by the forests and the log cabins and the newly plowed fields of the pioneer families.

The settlers had moved onto Shawnee land, so the Indians weren't friendly to any of them. Except Johnny Appleseed.

Once Johnny had found an Indian brave lying sick beside a stream in the woods. His horse had run off, and the Indian was too weak with fever to get back to his people.

Johnny knew which herbs would make the young brave well again. He gathered them and brought them back to the stream. He built a fire, fetched water, and boiled the herbs in his cooking pan. The young brave was soon able to walk again.

After that, the Shawnee were Johnny's friends. They thought he was a wise medicine man.

Johnny was glad to be the Indians' friend. But he worried about fights between the Shawnee and the settlers. The settlers were his friends, too. Johnny was sort of in the middle, and that's not an easy place to be. He wanted the Indians and the settlers to live peacefully. But that time was yet to come.

One night the settlers were wakened by a pounding on their cabin doors. It was Johnny Appleseed—but this time he had not come with seedling trees.

"Get to the Fort!" he shouted. "The Shawnee are coming!"

Half-asleep families hitched up horses and scrambled into wagons. They set out for Fort Mansfield as fast as they could. The sky was already red from the light of war fires, and there wasn't a moment to lose.

Johnny ran all night long, waking and warning the families.

But even when all the settlers had reached the Fort, the danger wasn't over. It was plain to see that there weren't enough people to fight off a big attack. The farmers stood ready with their rifles, and so did the Fort soldiers, but they were too few.

The Captain in charge of the Fort gathered everyone together. Firelight flickered on the log walls, and some of the little children began to cry. Their parents tried to hush and comfort them.

"The nearest help is the Fort at Mount Vernon," the Captain said in a grave voice.

He looked about into the faces of the soldiers and the faces of the frightened families who had come to the Fort for protection.

"If someone could get through to Mount Vernon," the Captain said, "and tell them we need help . . ."

There was a murmur among the people.

"Mount Vernon—that's thirty miles away!"

"It's too dangerous—no one could get through alive."

Johnny had been running all night, from cabin to cabin, warning the settlers. He was probably more than a mite tired, but he stepped right up and said, "I'll go. The Shawnee won't harm me."

He not only went, but he came the long, long way back again to guide the new troops through the forest. Maybe the Shawnee didn't see him. Maybe they did and wouldn't harm him, just as he said.

The Shawnee didn't want to fight all the soldiers and farmers that were at Fort Mansfield now. Instead, they went back to their camp, and the settlers got ready to go back to their cabins and fields.

As the settlers left the Fort, each one wrung Johnny's hand in a hearty handshake.

"There's no way to thank you," they said one by one.

The children waved goodbye from the wagons. "Come and see us, Johnny," they called.

"I'll be by," he promised. "But first I'm going to get a little sleep!"

Now that the danger was over, Johnny went into the quiet forest, stretched out on the ground with the sky for his roof, and rested.

As the years passed, peace did come between the Shawnee and the settlers.

And the wilderness land began to change. Small towns sprang up, with churches and

stores and mills. Blacksmith shops and inns
were readied for travelers. There were better
roads. And schools were built for the children.
Life was not as lonely or as hard for the
settlers.

And the land was beautiful, with apple orchards everywhere.

Johnny lived to be an old man. Before he died, the Ohio Valley was blooming with apple blossoms, and there was apple pie on the table in many a log cabin.

So whenever you bite into an apple—think of Johnny Appleseed. He wanted to help people, and that's just what he did all his life.